The National Poetry Series

The National Poetry Series was established in 1978 to publish five collections of poetry annually through five participating publishers: Persea Books, William Morrow & Co., the University of Illinois Press, Copper Canyon Press, and Viking Penguin. The manuscripts are selected by five poets of national reputation. Publication is funded by the Copernicus Society of America, James A. Michener, Edward J. Piszek, and The Lannan Foundation.

1991 Series

Good Hope Road, by Stuart Dischell
Viking Penguin
Selected by Thomas Lux

The Dig, by Lynn Emanuel
The University of Illinois Press
Selected by Gerald Stern

To Put The Mouth To, by Judith Hall
William Morrow & Co.
Selected by Richard Howard

As If, by James Richardson
Persea Books
Selected by Amy Clampitt

A Flower Whose Name I Do Not Know, by David Romtvedt
Copper Canyon Press
Selected by John Haines

GOOD
HOPE
ROAD

STUART DISCHELL

VIKING

VIKING
Published by the Penguin Group
Viking Penguin, a division of Penguin Books USA Inc.,
375 Hudson Street, New York, New York 10014, U.S.A.
Penguin Books Ltd, 27 Wrights Lane,
London W8 5TZ, England
Penguin Books Australia Ltd, Ringwood,
Victoria, Australia
Penguin Books Canada Ltd, 10 Alcorn Avenue, Suite 300,
Toronto, Ontario, Canada M4V 3B2
Penguin Books (N.Z.) Ltd, 182–190 Wairau Road,
Auckland 10, New Zealand

Penguin Books Ltd, Registered Offices:
Harmondsworth, Middlesex, England

First published in 1993 by Viking Penguin,
a division of Penguin Books USA Inc.

1 3 5 7 9 10 8 6 4 2

Page 79 constitutes an extension of this copyright page.

0-670-84822-0
CIP data available

Printed in the United States of America
Set in Janson
Designed by Brian Mulligan

This book is for Karen
and my mother and father

CONTENTS

all the black same I dance my blue head off
—John Berryman
"King David Dances"

GOOD HOPE ROAD

I

APARTMENTS

CARES

He cares about the trees this morning, he's concerned
That the lumber companies are cutting too many down.
He tells this to the man beside him on the porch
And to the nurse when she brings his medicine.
"Sayonara," he says and tilts it back. He thinks
About the rain forest and the Philippines and the months
Before Guadalcanal. He thinks about the holes
In the trees and his friends, and, although he knows
It's dumb, he thinks of trunks and branches and limbs.
"How will we breathe?" he asks the man beside him
Reading the funnies with a magnifying glass.
"It's okay for me. I've breathed all my life. But the kids
Will never get enough." The other man nods.
They go through this every morning—famine, wars,
Environmental destruction. He'd rather look
At Steve Canyon or what's happening with the girls in 3G.
And now it starts again: "Can you believe it?
They're tearing down the Amazon to grow french fries.
And your piece of garbage newspaper. Think of the trees.
Okay don't listen," he says and turns away. "Go read
Your crap. I'd sooner take one on the White House lawn."
He looks across the lawn, the horseshoe driveway,
And the old people on benches and gliders taking in
The good weather. "At least I care," he says to himself
This time, "about more than visits and grandchildren
And whether my teeth are hurting and they hurt plenty."
He shrugs, thinks to get up, then changes his mind.

He wonders when it was the willow got so leafy
And the maple this thick. He looks at his hands
He's known so long and the flesh of his forearms
Now hanging off the bone. Willow and maple,
Poplar, birch, oak, magnolia. He watches
A woman go by with her walker and some men
On metal sticks. He looks at the boards of the porch
And the furniture. "Don't cut a tree on my account.
Better I should burn or throw me naked into the ground."

NEEDS

She doesn't really want him, but sometimes she needs him.
Needs him the way she thinks a planet might need a star,
Though not so much for light as for bearing.
So at midnight, when he doesn't answer his phone,
She thinks of all the likely scenarios—visits
With friends, drinking sessions way into the night,
Accidents on the highway—but most of all
She imagines him in bed with another woman,
Him kissing her belly and breasts while the phone
Rings on the nightstand. But she's not exactly jealous
Of the sex—she knows she can have it too—
Or the fact that someone might be happier with him
Than she was able—she really believes she tried—
She's angry at his inaccessibility. She needs to think
He will always be available to answer her calls,
To tell her she is not going crazy, that the walls
Are not moving, that nobody really hates her.
Many times he asked to marry her and said that he would
Always be there. But she said no. She knows
It wouldn't work, for what she's attracted to
Is not his hands or heart or mind or face.
It's as if he's a place, a safe place, a safe
Where she can store all the doubts she's saved
And does not have to share them with anybody else.
But she doesn't want to hide herself in there.
She wants to go out dancing and date the best guys
Who ask her to lift her skirts in the wild fandango.

She needs him because she trusts him and he already knows
What could be called the truth about her. She thinks
How money might feel looked after by a guard.
She needs him now because she wants to tell him
About what was not a dream but her vision: she saw them
Together on a high bridge. Her stomach stuck out as though
She were pregnant. One by one she handed him kittens.
He kissed each one as he dropped it in a weighted sack,
And he said a prayer before he threw them into the river.

HATES

He hates to wake up in the morning alone,
What it's like to squeeze juice for one,
To stumble around in only pajama bottoms
With no one to admire his recent tan
Or explicate his significant dreams.
Sure, he's glad not to be scolded for stuff
In his eye or the place he missed shaving.
But those admonishments become endearments
Over the time it takes for the coffee to drip.
He hates the way time fools him and distorts
Righteousness into guilt and blame, makes him
Eat the yoghurt she liked even though he finds it
Sour. And why should he worry about his health
Now when there's no one to be in shape for?
Oh, he knows there're others waiting to be tricked
In and out of love, the anonymous someone
For whom he will assume all the qualities
He's never had. But it's all in fun, isn't it?
Men are jerks and women are hostile,
And anchored to its dish the butter lies
Too cold to spread. There are toast crumbs
Inside the toaster that catch fire every time
The button is pressed. The floor needs sweeping,
The windows cleaning. And who is that guy
In the neighbor's apartment. He hates it
When the equilibrium is disturbed, like when
They spray for roaches in only one unit.

He hates it and he's said so, not just
To be a pain in the ass but to let them know
He's not someone to be pushed around.
He's quit jobs for imagined slights,
Walked out of restaurants because of waiters'
Attitudes, told off the drivers of public
Conveyances who were not in fact "safe,"
"Courteous," and "efficient." He flexes
In the mirror and punches his solar plexus.
He times his eggs before he cracks them.
He hates the bosses and oppressors,
Votes only for losing candidates,
Knows that he will never be president
Or arrive at anyone's concept of heaven.

WISHES

Her car isn't turning over and she wishes
She had a new one. Once she had a boyfriend
Who wore a silly cap when he fixed things—
Sometimes with parts left over—but they didn't
Like each other's friends so now he's gone.
She wishes things didn't end the way they do.
She wonders if it's like this for everyone.
"It's the sex thing," her mother would say,
As if there were any way around it. So her Mom
Remarried the year after Dad died. She wishes
She didn't have stepsisters and that her room
In the old house could stay the way she left it.
George is okay, though. Never asks her to call
Him Dad. Not that she would. She wishes George
Were here now because he could keep the man
From the garage from cheating her. The tow truck
Pulls down the block. A guy in blue coveralls
Opens the hood, clucks his tongue, adjusts wires.
"It's the cables," he tells her, "just loose cables,"
And charges thirty bucks. She watches his face
In the tow truck's side mirror as he drives
Away. She strokes her hair. Not that she's interested,
But he looks somehow reliable, like a guy who
Drinks beer at the VFW. Her ex-professor called
Last night because his wife's away. It's clear
He only sees her when it's safe for him.
Tonight they'll go to a restaurant on the road

And later back to her place for bed. She wishes
He'd stop all his lecturing. Everything's become
A subject for his lectures—food and wine
And politics and sex. And really he could use
Some study in the latter. She wishes she were older
Or younger, wishes the sky were a little calmer,
That it wouldn't rain on her driving errands,
That she wasn't so late for her appointment,
That the car's problem was really only the cables,
That it could be summer faster, that what she had been
Waiting for all her life would finally begin to happen,
That she would know it when it was happening,
And that when it happened it would not disappoint her, ever.

CHEATS

When the girls at the register cheat her, when they bag
The can of lentil soup on top of her bread and fruit,
When the prices on the packages don't match up,
Rotten berries buried in the center of the pint,
The chopped meat brown on the side that faces down,
The frankfurters green below their plastic wrapping,
In a rage she circles the items on the receipt
And packs them up to take them back. At the market
She shouts for the manager, a man used to complaints.
He answers her in a booming voice, thinking she can't
Hear him as he goes over each of the products and shakes
His head, disgusted with her or the moldy fruit.
"Good for you," says a man who is cutting coupons
At the courtesy booth and pats her on the shoulder.
"They're all a bunch of crooks." But the fellow behind her,
Waiting for his check to be approved, clucks his tongue.
"It's not just the money it's the principle of the thing,"
She says as she examines the coins and bills.
"You should pay me for my time." The manager smiles
Down on her, an old lady with a blue cloud of hair.
From behind the high booth he is a giant, a sun,
A Supreme Court Justice, all the occupations
He might have been. He'd like to tell this lady
And the whole store about his wife's medical bills,
The problems with his car, his daughter's drug habit.
He'd like to shout it over the loudspeaker
As if he were announcing a special on Fig Newtons.

He'd like to rip off his apron and leap into the clouds
Like Superman. He'd like to get into the pants
Of the punked-out stock boy. Then just punch
The time clock once and for all. Punch it for real
Like they do in cartoons. "Have a good day," he says
Because it is Wednesday. "Have a safe weekend," he'd say
If today were Friday. The woman sighs and says nothing.
She walks past the bag boys and gum machines, the rubber
Hen on a nest of prizes, the wooden pony, and the bottle
Redemption center. She steps toward the doors and they open
For her in an instant; they open as if by magic.

BUDDIES

His life seems dull so he tells a friend's story
As if it were his own. He tells it so many times
And with such conviction, he thinks it happened
To him. Some, who know the story and the friend,
Try to comprehend the reasoning of his falsehood.
Others, who hear the story, doubt the friend.
The world of acquaintances divides into camps,
And at parties where neither is invited
Discussions break into fisticuffs and furniture
Gets smashed—butter sauce down a woman's dress.
All this while the man and his friend are ignorant
To the efforts of their interpreters. The two meet
After work for games of chance then to drink
And eat at their favorite bar. Alternately one buys
The other's meal and the other leaves the tip.
It's a system they've invented over years of friendship,
Like one hand washing the other, you scratching
My back and me scratching yours, and other sayings
They are fond of saying. Most nights they talk
About their childhoods and current difficulties.
They describe in detail what they think and feel
Concerning the waitress's rear end. They're buddies,
Pals, boon companions. And they both are named Jerry.
Small wonder there could exist some confusion.
One day Jerry's wife receives a letter
From the partisans of the other Jerry. Shocked,
She acts as if her Jerry has been unfaithful.

"Jerry," she confronts him, "Jerry has been telling
Your stories as if they are his own." "Well,
Maybe they are," answers the amicable Jerry.
"But this one is about us and the first time
We did it," she replies. "I wouldn't know
How he found out about that." Jerry winks and says,
"Jerry's not a happy person, so if he tells
A story that approximates the events of my life
And this gives him pleasure in a world of misery,
Then what's the harm?" "Because it's my story, too."
"Then you ought to tell it. In the scheme of things
Our lives are a joke, and we Jerrys are its comedians."

THE GENIUS

He feels the world will one day absolve him
And might even prove he was always right.
He feels he's a realist and considers himself
Modest, so he doesn't talk about it much
Unless he's drunk. He still holds boyhood daydreams
Of heroic acts—pulling children from a fiery bus—
Yet now transformed with a grown-up need
For vindication. He feels the world should pay him
More attention, that others less worthy have been
Given positions of wealth and prestige.
In his new fantasies he's stronger and taller
And instead of kids he rescues the Nobel Committee.
Sure, he's read Walter Mitty and discussed
His problem with his ex-wife's therapist,
Who looked as though he could use some delusions
Of his own. One summer he tried to be a writer.
Although he enjoyed discussing his vocation,
He had tremendous difficulty deciding on genre.
Was he to be a novelist or autobiographer?
In the end, of course, he abandoned it.
He feels he would never have found a publisher.
So, he imagines saving a convention of publishers.
He feels he is brave and noble but when questioned
He cannot recall any brave or noble action.
But he feels he has the capacity for brave
And noble actions, and that's what counts.
He knows his friends hope someone will call

His hand, that crushed he might be easier
To deal with and contain like a pineapple
Without crown or core, or a can of corn.
He remembers how his father would come home
Beaten from a day at work, how their dinner
Would be silent and afterwards his father
Would sit all night in the darkened den
Lighting one cigarette from the stub
Of another. He feels he should have saved
His father from the creditors and suicide
At fifty. "Dad," he says as he prizes
The old man's coffin, "skeleton come alive."

OUT OF THE DUST

She finds interesting stuff everywhere they go.
Say on a road in Mexico or Ohio, she'll pick
Something out of the dust and it will be
An arrowhead sticking out, just waiting for her.
Or swimming in the surf she'll surface
With a crusty doubloon in each hand. What he finds
Is broken glass, a bottle cap, or the little plastic tips
From popular cigars. It's infuriating
To have such a sister, how after she claims
She's broke and has borrowed for weeks,
She finds a twenty in an old coat pocket
And spends it without consulting him. But it's not just
Stuff she finds, it's what she sees on a car ride
Or a simple walk in the woods. Although he knows
For a fact there haven't been moose in the state
For fifty years, she'll say she's seen one.
And when he goes out to show her up, they won't find
The moose but he'll have to agree the hoofprints
She finds are indisputably mooselike. It's like this
With locations of nude beaches, otherwise invisible
Hitchhikers, or her knowledge that his fiancée
Was married once before. How she finds out,
He's never been able to figure. Prescience or intuition,
She denies possessing either. She says that finding
Is a matter of seeing. "Remember how Dad would take us
On walks to the river? You would watch the sculls
Go by, or the reflection of clouds on the water.

All the while I'd be staring into the grass
Until I could almost see the roots and I'd count
As many blades as I could. Or, looking at Dad's head
I'd see the pattern he was going bald. When he smoked
I read the matchbook name. I found out long ago
About the accident and that his business
Was going broke. It's no trick or luck. What started
As a little game has become my way of life."

TAKES

He takes an inventory of his life, at first
It's the people he's harmed in- or un-
Intentionally, then the acts he's performed
Out of selfishness, ingratitude, or malice.
An eleven-year-old Oswald with a BB gun,
He remembers hiding in the eaves of the house,
The spun fiberglass wool and the attic window.
He remembers the startled look on the neighbor's face
As he pictures him running round and round
Before returning to his evening mowing.
One Mischief Night he broke into houses
And stole someone's pillow. So much for youth!
At college he vandalized the president's office
And purged friends from revolutionary committees.
One summer he grew a Stalinesque moustache.
At sexual relations his record is no better,
But was he the betrayed or the betrayer?
It takes all day to make his list.
He tries to leave nothing out and the more
He takes down the worse he feels, having
Exhausted all the deadly sins and probed
Deeply into white lies. So he begins to
Figure his basic statistics, like the ones
On the backs of baseball cards. He reckons
The number of hamburgers he's eaten,
The french fries, hot dogs, and BLTs.
The quantity of beers consumed in cans,

In bottles and on tap—lifetime totals
And yearly average. How will I ever finish,
He thinks—fingernails clipped, hairs lost,
Pints of sperm. The times I've said yes and no,
Elevators ridden, buttons buttoned, steps taken,
Bowels moved, in- and ex-halations, and the wavings
Of good-bye.

LIKES

He likes to walk in the forest alone, go days
Without seeing another person and not care
Where the deer path takes him. He's given up
Maps in favor of wandering. He likes the word
Aimless and the birdsongs he knows are important.
He likes bramble and thicket, stand and riprap.
He likes to watch the fat robin at work in the morning
And the gray owl rise through the trees in the starlight.
He likes the pattern the light makes through the leaves.
He believes the cattails are supplicants to the wind.
With his favorite stick he gauges the river.
"Mark Twain," he calls out to no one in particular.
Sometimes he wonders if a search party follows him,
Bloodhounds pursuing his escape from the well-meaning
Friends and relations who would like him committed
To a counter job in the family business.
"Thoreau," his uncle calls him. "The Noble Savage,"
His brother gibes. Aren't they smart enough
To see he doesn't want to be anybody or anything?
He's never understood the holy admonition
About being a lily of the field—because he wouldn't
Want to stay rooted to one place. He wants to clarify
The concept of getting lost. This is my occupation,
He thinks, shaking a stone from inside his boot.
He likes to eat fungus and berries and the little apples
The deer can't reach. He likes to walk through the rain

And stand straight up in a grove of pines.
He likes to strip off his clothes and sleep in the sun
Or touch the petals where they rise. He says,
"Why not be pollen before we're dust?"

WORKS

Because they have no family he works
At their relationship, this thing they have made
Between them like a child. Because it does not
Have a name, he would like to give it one,
Something from antiquity, as enduring
As bread but without the getting stale.
It would be made from hammered gold.
It would have wings and it would have a mouth.
It would delight him all day, just by thinking
About it waiting, like a pet that was glad
To see him. He would shine it up and take it out.
He would place it on the shelf above their bed,
And they would care for it, oh, care for it,
More than they have anything else. Several times
A day he calls her where she works. "I'm working,"
She says the way a person might say, "I'm full."
He knows his emptiness, that all he can offer are meals
And hands and maybe a weekend somewhere fine,
A kiss upon waking, a breathing pillow
She can hold through the nights she cannot sleep.
He floats in the current, her preoccupied stare,
Treading the air of the gulf between them
Content that it is not an ocean. He drowns
In the logic of his longing while she pulls at
Her long black hair. She takes the woolen sweater

She gave him for Christmas and unknots each stitch
Until the skein curls round her hands.
He would make a new garment for them to wear,
And they would work triumphant in their city.

PLANS

She plans to be a writer one day and live in the City of Paris,
Where she will describe the sun as it rises over Buttes-Chaumont.
"Today the dawn began in small pieces, sharp wedges of light
Broke through the clouds." She plans to write better than this
And is critic enough to know "sharp wedges" sound like cheese.
She plans to live alone in a place that has a terrace
Where she will drink strong coffee at a round white table.
Her terrace will be her café and she will be recognized
By the blue-smocked workers of the neighborhood, the concierges,
The locals at the *comptoir* of the tabac down the block,
And the girl under the green cross of the apothecary shop.
She plans to love her apartment where she will keep
Just one flower in a blue vase. She already loves the word apart-
Ment, whose halves please her when she sees them breaking
The line in her journal. She plans to learn the roots
Of French and English words and will search them out
As if she were hunting skulls in the catacombs.
On her walls she'll hang a timetable of the great events
Of Western History. She will read the same twenty books
As Chaucer. Every morning she will make up stories. . . .
She looks around her Brighton room, at the walls,
The ceiling, the round knob of the rectangular door.
She listens to the voices of the neighbor's children.
A toilet flushes, then the tamp of cigarette on steel,
The flint flash of her roommate's boyfriend's lighter.

When she leaves she plans to leave alone, and every
Article she will carry, each shoe, will be important.
Like an architect she will plan this life, as once
The fortune in a cookie told her: *Picture what you wish*
To become, if you wish to become that picture.

II

HOUSEHOLD GODS

THE JETTY

Like a ruin it was hard to figure
Who quarried, carried, and assembled here
The steady rocks, familially touching,
Inextricable as the good men of Calais.

A Stonehenge at low tide, to a small boy
Their peaks glowered, the salt-sloped
Windbeaten sides were pyramids for climbing
And the slime-green seaward angles

Dangerously crustaceous. The ancients
Dwelled here—the rare red crab,
A chariot-driven, archaic warrior,
Defended his moment before extinction.

The runic mussels and barnacles clung
Like some indigenous peoples
After the looting of their kingdoms.
I was Cortez. I was Balboa. I was any

Fool in bushclothes and a monocle,
Preposterous as the rocks were ponderous.
Followed by a gang of bearers,
I took my place among the idols.

Protagonists from every age
Consorted in this unpacked heaven;
Emperors deployed their legions,
The shapes of clouds in transmigration.

When the evening tide came in
Covering the temples like a jungle
The boulders provided vast plateaus,
Stepping stones across the archipelago.

Then these were the sirens' islands,
Lost beaches of the starved discoverers,
Where in small wooden boats
Vikings and Saints might both set out.

Farthest at sea, where the waves broke,
Stood that northern castle
Upon whose parapets the future spoke,
While sea water soaked my ankles numb

And a woman's voice kept calling me home.

BETWEEN TWO STORMS

It was the hour between the dog and the wolf
The sun in the far corner   the half-moon rising
I was out   walking again   the iced-over
Unreflective street brittle underheel   there was
Something I wanted to wish for but I could not
Find it among the scattered notions   I could not
Cough it up like a bone in my throat for it was
Already dissolving   a half-eaten lozenge
Bitten   bitter   broken   I complain too much
Can't keep a secret   try not to tell myself anything
Anymore   just take it in like breath   the streets
The traffic   the glances people see with
Before passing   O   a star fell in the sky
Far away   in the yellow lights of a living room
A woman was   closing out the night   leaning forward
Over the sill   pulling down the shade   I kept her
Longer than I saw her   I kept her so I would remember
If ever I forgot what a woman looks like   leaning over
Closing out the night   pulling down the shade   not
Abruptly or slowly but evenly   decisively   as if
All patterns and reflexes of her life brought us
To this one moment   a brownstone apartment   the back
Of her hand facing the window   her palm inward
Fingers bent in an absent wave   the crease of a lifeline
Farewell   the old year was done   the first square
Of a new calendar filling in   I kept on   I had
Little else to do   I was not expected anywhere

It was good to be   insignificant   undesired   loose
As a leaf scuttling along the pavement   a bit out
Of season but still here   watching the cloudy evidence
My occupation of the cold free air

MIRRORS AND SHADOWS

If I could pick a day
The way one picks a flower,
I would take a Friday when I was twenty,
Having cut class to work on my car,
A beer sitting on the trunk,
The sun reflecting on the windshield,
Hippie girls passing in their bedspread dresses.

I know it was all for effect,
This life of mine.
Everything I did was for someone
To notice—the clothes, the shoes, the car, the hair,
The way my bicep pouted from a rolled-up sleeve,
Wrench in my hand, cigarette burning on the fender.

But the audience was looking elsewhere.
So I learned to love mirrors and shadows.
I stood outside galleries and concert halls.
I carried books with difficult titles
And learned phrases in foreign languages
Should ever a shadow wish to speak with me.

I don't know how it came to happen,
Maybe yesterday during one of those slowed-down seconds,
That finally it no longer mattered.

I didn't feel free, though,
And I didn't feel dead.
It was not like the space after climax
Or rising from surgery.
I don't believe it's wisdom,
Although it seems like knowledge,
The happiness of waking in one's own bed.

If days were shapely as clouds
And each appeared different,
Should you take the time to notice,
You might envision yourself up there,
Nimbus among the cumulus,
A little more special some days than others,
Like a favorite among the pines on the hillside,
As seen from the highway on which you are traveling,
Or waiting there among the persons in warm coats at the station.

LIGHT INDUSTRY

Volcanic inactivity,
The woman beside me is sleeping.
She trembles so deep she does not shake.
Her face is creased by furrows on the sheet.
Waking should heal last night's dreams.
Outside, solitary drivers
Begin with coffee cups, lunch pails, briefcases.
It's morning and the day's all possibilities.

Maybe the noon sun makes the day unpleasant
Or a shadow overwhelms me on the street,
A sexual *duende*, tall, melancholy, thin,
Wearing the eye makeup of violent death.
She says, "You may take me home, now or later,
You may take me home." But it isn't enough
To be naked—I want to hear her stories,
What lovers were before me, what they did.

And a woman tells me, "The president screws poorly,
Always abstracted by the light on the wall,
Always desiring some mythic woman, and worse
He loves the memory of lovemaking more
Than the body itself." Maybe she says this
For my benefit. "The workers and professionals
Are no better with their clinical and raw approaches,
And even you, my love, are no better
With your hands that never relax, shoulders

Tense as a bridge over a swollen river,
And your dreams and grinding teeth."

So I go visit the old young men, young old men,
World-weary early, who have won great honors
In their time, long or brief, is or was.
Businessman artists, journeyman liars,
Who spark and convalesce, who scorn
My walks and wandering and in one voice say,
"Sit down, Stuart." Across the street
A man throws rock salt on the pavement
The way a farmer tosses feed to chickens.

GOOD HOPE ROAD

I had been thinking of Good Hope Road,
Starting like a river's source
In a dusty field, a sylvan lane,
Or a slum street in the moist and neglected
Heart of the Great American City.
Good Hope Road: that name alone
Takes me from suburbia to Alpha Centauri,
Quick as the once-taught *World of the Future* . . .
Good Hope Road: I was a boy there delivering papers,
A hitchhiker, a convict working a jackhammer.
I drove a Firebird, a bread truck, a hearse.
I carried trash from the pretty houses.
I was a deer strayed from the wood lots,
A salamander crossing the midsummer evening,
And the one that didn't mean to run them down.
This is how the road began, why the highway
Got paved. On a rainy night in Dayton, Ohio,
A hooker in a bar told me, "I was fifteen
And walking with my sister down Good Hope Road
When a car with out-of-state plates slowed down."
Or, riding in a Buick with a real estate agent
Showing me homes, he confided, "Good Hope Road:
There's no finer place in the whole town."
And in the jail where I'm kept overnight
On D & D charges, my cellmate, whistle-toothed,
Chain-smoking, said, "Good Hope Road:
I been there. Cops'll bust your ass."

Good Hope Road: I have followed your lines
From the wetlands to the growers' vines.
I have seen the mileage marked. Good Hope Road:
Who named you? who pounded your first sign
In the dirt and dreamed at once of somewhere else?
Good Hope Road: America remains in your phrasing,
A cartoon of the land as it never was,
Where the sun smiles in its corner of the sky
While jet trails go loop-de-loo . . .
Nevertheless, having said what I have said
About where I have been, strap on my back
Or steering wheel in my hands, in the not
Yet risen dawn of another earthbound day,
I will set out again down that same road,
My hope companionable among the travelers.

OLD HORSES

Old horses
Come quickly to the fence,
Not out of friskiness
But out for reward.

Their veined faces
Scare me a little
And the top lips they pull back
Show large yellow teeth.

I would be afraid
To blow in their nostrils
The way my sister-in-law does
To make them feel safe.

Old horses
Do not like me so well.
My gestures are abrupt
And they flick their tails.

When they return to the field
They keep me in their field
Of vision. I think
They must think

I am like the dog
From the farm next door.
Or else they have seen
My unpretty soul.

HAWKWEED

If, in a field of hawkweed,
You rose from the Indian blanket
Where you had been loafing over
A sandwich and a foreign wine,
And the clouds were slowly grazing
Like ten sheep in a meadow,
And you were thinking not remembering
The girl whose shape is indelible
Beneath the sandwich you had forgotten
But not the shapely bottle;
If, in a field of hawkweed,
You counted on the rise the singular trees
Folding under the wing of the mountain's shadow;
If, in a field of hawkweed,
If, in a field of hawkweed,
The real hawk flew over its flowering name.

GREEN MOUNTAIN RAIN
(To R. P. W.)

I

The arthritic postures of the apple trees.
The faces turning over in the leaves.
Like cows lying down in the pastures,
The living sense the coming rain.
So let it rain. Better not to curse
The forces over which there is no control.

II

Lazy one day I lay on the big worn rock
And dangled my heels in the moving brook.
Above my eyes, in the tall sugarbush,
The sun tangled in the tree's branches
(An effortless image but not my own).
Bump on a log, rock on a rock, there I was
Finally doing something I was good at—
Idly turning the pages of a borrowed book.

III

I climbed the woods to Stratton Peak
On the blind side of that dread resort
The developers built to twit your days.
I was fearful. Someone had laughed
Because I knew nothing of bushcraft.
Soon my fear opened into terror,

And I wished you had never told me
Bears get drunk on fermented apples.

IV

I remember your story of your friend,
Your subject, a man so bold at college.
How you saw him two score later:
Living in Chicago as lonely as God.

In the flyleaf below your name,
You inscribed your last fiction:
"There are many errors here,
But I cannot correct them all."

HISTORY LESSONS
(Henry Adams)

I sat on the side of the world
Trying to find my place.
The classroom globe spun on its axis:
New World, Old World, continents, nations, states.
I could almost see my house and street.
I thought, "This is what God sees when he looks down."

And we look up to him, the old schoolmaster,
Seated at his desk in front of the room,
Urging us to be good—a virgin, a lamb—
Scaring us to work with his dreadful flame.

Like Grandfather in the library,
He wants to be fair, will pause
In the busyness of his days
To walk the boy to school.

*   *   *

The silence of a woman's absence.

An empty house, the spoken and unspoken blame.
I'd like to say I did the best I could for her,
But there was my work to be done.
And there was always but.

The honest historian does not write
Of his own times. When I was young
I wanted to be objective. But
There were family scores to settle.
And Madison and Jefferson.

The silence of a woman's absence.

After thirty years
I cannot write the portrait of my lady.

*   *   *

Fenestration, a word as ugly as the thing
Is beautiful. Mont St.-Michel.
Relics of rose windows.

The Lord of Light leaping into shadow,
Hurling himself forward and upward,
Vanquishing infidels
And Saxons.

The knights support Duke William
And The Bastard supports his king.
The crypts support the halls
And the halls support the nave.

At Coutances, moving up the tower,
The square becomes the octagon,
The octagon the spire.

Holy is our architecture,
The marriage of human aspirations,
To love our art in God.

So the historian of another age
Or planet, who unearths the statues
From what was once this world,
Might find among commercial ruins

On earth there lived a people with wings.

MAGIC FATHERS

One appears in a snowstorm just as you're worrying
how you will get home.

Another in costume puts you on his knee.

Another buys a new car so you'll pass your driver's test.

And one crawls out from under the bed, having chased
the goblins away.

Oh, magic fathers, I summon you in the bleak time
when the rum has given out and the glass has left circles
on the table.

Oh, magic fathers, you will buff them out, you will carry
us upstairs, you will watch us sleep.

For you are the dollar under the pillow.

You are the blanket, the wall, the window.

You in your anger the wrecker's ball.

FOR ROBERT MAURER

There were a circle of us then
Reading Homer in the sun,

The drugged among us in the August heat
Imagining what plants Ulysses ate.

Not far, on a mound of grass,
Stood the granite cenotaph:

"STUDENTS, BE ASHAMED TO DIE
UNTIL YOU HAVE WON SOME VICTORY FOR HUMANITY."

Amazing, Mann's words were left alone.
Beyond them, Fuller's geodesic dome,

Crosshatched like a series of monkey bars
Through which at night we watched the stars.

Our mood was all very Sixties,
Though it was already the early Seventies,

And we had not yet reached our twenties
Except for you, Bob, in your fifties.

Your boys were bearded, your girls without bras,
And some believed that clothes were bourgeois,

This further connivance of the ruling classes
To estrange the always idolized masses.

False consciousness, we termed it then.
You resembled a chicken, our mother hen,

A man I worshipped for having met Auden,
Now guiding us through the Mediterranean.

Then it happened, the sun's yolk cracked.
A dog pissed yellow down your back.

The last class you would hold outdoors.
—Treacherous, you learned, these disciples of yours.

SAND

Not a mirror but a pane of glass.
As if I could walk beside myself . . .

Striped blankets on the shore,
Low tide, clam water,
An awning bucking in the wind,
The horse made of air kicking its heels.

Picture the sun in 1962.
The President in Ray-Bans.
My room: red, white, and blue.
Heavy red cotton bedspread.
Cornflakes for breakfast
And raisin toast.

"Shit," said my father
Entering the kitchen
Where I was doing nothing
About his coffee boiling over.
My father with a towel
Wrapped around the waist of his suit pants.
My father
Interrupted from his shaving
While I did nothing.
The grounds rising up through the percolator.

Not a mirror but a pane of glass.
Did you hear that dog bark?
Are we out of milk?

I had these friends once
Who broke into houses.
They wanted me to come along,
But I was scared my mother would die.

Snowdrifts against the bulkheads,
The beach like a frozen tundra,
And I, having just seen Zhivago,
Made my forced march
Where no footprints went before me.
I liked Yuri's fur hat
And the writing paper in his desk.
Someone was a Communist.
I couldn't imagine then
Loving more than one woman.

Not a mirror but a pane of glass.

The floors were carpeted,
The furniture modern.

Father and Mother,
Smelling good, all dressed up,
Sharkskin and sequins.
And where are you going, my darlings?
The Club Harlem, The 500, The Bamboo?

I waited for them to come home
(And they always did)
As now I wait for you.

Truth is, I never grew up.
Having no wife or child,
I have kept myself the child,
With the same ghosts and demons,
And the sound of blood when I close my eyes.

     ✱   ✱   ✱

One summer I collected bottles,
The whole backyard filled with them—
Coke and White Rock and Hires and Ma's,
Pepsi and Yoo-Hoo and Canada Dry.
At the Acme they paid two cents,
But Gertz only gave me a penny.

Sometimes we'd release all the parakeets,
And they would sit on my brother's head.
There are pictures of this. I can show you
The main cage, the hospital cage,
And the vacation cage like the hotel
My parents stayed at in the mountains.

Mrs. Don-na-hee
(I don't know how to spell her name)
Took care of me sometimes for weeks.
And Ernestine came in the afternoons.
Father brought home swizzle sticks
And Mother's souvenirs.
So, if you go away, be sure to bring me something back.

*   *   *

But I forgot to tell you about the ocean.
It was there all the time the way I now have traffic.
Summer evenings my parents would swim together.
It was the closest thing I've seen to their making love.
I think when they got out past the breakers,
They looked like porpoises in the swells.
But I still haven't told you about the ocean.
It was gray and green and sometimes blue.
The way I've seen your eyes get.

Not a mirror but a pane of glass.
I know I have disappointed you.

    ✳   ✳   ✳

Other summer evenings,
Rising crocodillic from his nap,
My otherwise restless father said,
"Let's go for a ride,"
And so we would ride
Over the bridges and marsh roads.
It was then I realized we lived on an island,
Though I thought it should be the other way around.

The toll taker's name was Broadwater.
My father always kidded him,
A repetition I could anticipate,
As when passing the cemetery he'd ask,
"How many dead people are buried there?"
"All of them," I would answer.

Boatyards and docks rushed by
The side windows, terrapin shells
Along the roadside like broken hatboxes,
The diving birds in the marshland.
Then the quiet in our thoughts: Mother
At her easel, Father in Mexico,
My brother at school.

You see it means something to me
That I should remember them better.

Was I the heart of that body?

    *   *   *

Or merely one of the eyes,
Singular, uncoupled, without much
Depth perception, the way the car
With one headlight comes at us,
Driving at seventy on a road meant for thirty,
The beery song of the passing occupants.

    *   *   *

Not a mirror but a pane of glass.

You can still feel the tin
On Lucy the Elephant, a century old,
Moved from Gertz's beach lot
To her new incarnation as The Elephant Museum.
And Gertz's children, returned to the Pine Barrens,
Sell souvenirs of the Jersey Devil.

I was not that tortured child kept in the house.
I loved my nest on the living room couch.
The grown-ups smoking cigarettes then.
Moving lips and talking tongues.
And five-dollar bills slipped to me
From an uncle's hand.

What does it mean to be the sum
Of all their parts,
To sleep in the sweetness of the family plot?

     *   *   *

In my dreams we are always at the house.
It makes sense, the way dreams do,
For where else should we be except our house,
Where else could we matter?

Did I tell you it was white and stucco?
I don't think I've said the word stucco in a long time
And never in a context other than our house.
Stucco, some Italian invention funny to the touch.

There were hydrangea bushes in the front yard,
Pink and blue, till a storm when I was seven
Pulled them through the garden wall.
We were so scared of hurricanes then,

By the time they touched Cape Hatteras
We had bivouacked in the attic,
Where my father brought in the news
On the local band of his shortwave radio.

What he listened to
Those other nights
On the overseas stations,
I can only imagine:

Spy versus spy,
From the top step
I watched him
Wearing those headphones.

     *   *   *

Not a mirror but a pane of glass.
You would think I could look both ways.

My first recorded words:
Change mind.
Said in the supermarket
After running down the aisle:
Change mind.
So many times now:

Change mind.
So many changes.
And then the irreversible.

*   *   *

You must be weary, having listened
Without telling of your own terrain.
I know there are hillocks on your mind,
Certain lakes for swimming,
The familial forms that flesh out
From the shadows, flower in the brain,
Your own homecoming, an auction of memories.

Hold me now,
The white spread opens like a new world.

*   *   *

Working obliquely and from time to time,
I have written this poem by ignoring it,
As seashore plants are always hardy,
Having endured the spells induced
By weather or the whim of a householder's hand.

In this way it can be said
The Narrator also is God,
A Maker-of-Souls, a Taker-Away,
The Grim & Ultimate Puppeteer
In some Medieval Passion.

But we do not fight each other for the sun,
Though we have sometimes met as warriors on a plane,
Our geometry is proximate and enough,
The sand on which we sleep our dream of love.

Not a mirror but a pane of glass.
What would you have me ask for if not this

Picture window or sliding door
Through which the past plays

In continuous repertory, like the sea

Whose speaking parts, the waves,
Break the silence into sand.

FOOL'S GOLD

Remember the days before our troubles
And how, if not likely, we were possible,
The way discoveries are still possible,
If not likely.

Outside the bedroom window,
Leaves lifted in the wind
Like butterflies on the wing.
At night, a new planet rose.

And the god for whom we waited
Dusted our sleeping bodies.
Oh, there were many stories to tell.

I recall the moment,
Exact as a razor,
We slipped from the wire
Severing past from future.

Entwined in the catch
Like netted dolphins
We thrashed till we were mute.

I speak to you this morning
As I walk the dry riverbed,
Looking for arrowheads in my path,
Pocketing rocks worth saving.

Pyrite is fool's gold,
And the one who values it
Displaces something else
As he shouts to heaven like Archimedes.

"Eureka," I said when I touched you.
"Eureka," I said when I lost you.
—My bright lessons.

SOUVENIR

The night we played
Our nervous game of cards,
I lost every hand,
Sat naked on the single bed
Till you took off your clothes.
We were from the same resort—
Boarded houses and beach hotels
Where the shipwrecked return to shore,
Faithful and poor.
Love, I'll gamble
The angelic stone heralds
Wept in the rubble
When the Traymore fell:
The cranes lifted up
Their piping for salvage.
Little left for us
Of that city we knew.
The night you stripped
Your dress whispered
To the floor. Your mother slept.
The lightbulbs were bare.

Speak to me now,
Snowstorm in a glass jar.

THE BULLETIN BOARD

Odd in this world of ersatz to find the beige expanse of cork,
After they had removed the layers of postcards and photographs
Of what seemed to her, being younger, a lifetime.

Some were menus and wine lists of favorite European restaurants
Where he had dined with her, the other her, while the present
Her was still in high school.

"How can you be jealous," he said, and she wasn't because these
Memories were not hurtful to either—they had just remained
Always in place on the bulletin board.

But now they were repainting the kitchen, stripping the wallpaper
Together, hanging new towel racks, papering the drawers and shelves,
And scrubbing behind the refrigerator.

Looking at the bulletin board the next morning, he saw the cork
Had somehow healed itself, that there were no tears or pinholes
Or visible signs of previous usage.

He thought of that lot in his hometown, where once a house
Had stood with detailed sills and lintels and how after he returned,
Though he never learned the reason,

The house was gone and in its place a field of grass.

WOMEN IN THE CITY, WOMEN IN THE RAIN

Because I have seen women in the city
Take off their shoes in summer to walk barefoot
Through puddles in the rain, I know I can be happy.

One holds two bananas in her hand; another, black boats.
And one other, a little goofy, wears hers like a hat.
I think it's time we should all wear hats,
Put on our hats and go find these women in the rain.

THE CORNER

Whatever her name was
I no longer remember
Except the waiting
At that sharp corner
The trucks would turn too quickly,
So I would have to be cautious,
I with my grim face
And knowledge.

A soldier at his post
Long after the war,
I stood there waiting
Because nobody told me.
Not the friend who lied
To protect her.
Not the friend who lied
To protect me.
And especially not her
Whatever her name was.

I remember her breasts.
They were high and fierce,
A terror to behold
As my nervous hands
Fumbled with the catch.
My mistake:
My hands were weak.

She hated weakness.
She loved to smirk.

When the phone would ring
In a nearby shop,
I leaned to the door,
Hoping for my call.
When she called my name
Two syllables were three.
Three was her number,
The third in shadow,
Waiting like me.

Waiting
Till the parking meters expired,
My watch battery died,
And the awnings folded.
I wished for a hammock,
Shaved ice, a straw,
Some comfort from the nothing
Like the sound of her heels
And the bruise of her kiss.

Whatever her name was,
Sometimes when passing
That same sharp corner
I see myself there

With my knowledge,
Looking like a man
Who deserves forgetting,
Wearing his best clothes
And too much cologne.

THE MESSAGE

"I lie in my bed with my fears as you might lie
With a husband or wife, or lie that you fear at all
And march eagerly into the world. I know
This is just another one of your deceptions,
The functional lie of your existence. Once
I was like you. I held another's hand.
I pressed for strength. I let myself be touched.
Now no one can touch me. I have made it clear
I do not wish to be touched. Mornings I read,
Evenings I watch television. It's the afternoons
That trouble me. They obligate me.
They make me want to be like you again.
But it's not far to the take-out corner,
The dry cleaner where I leave my bedclothes
And outfits, the pharmacy where I get my medication.
I used to try to sleep through the afternoons,
But that was worse—I could not sleep at night.
I imagined you sleeping and it seemed to me obscene,
The short snores and eyelid flutters, the words
You might utter, recognizable only in your dreams.
And you might tell them to me. I never dream.
If I were near you, I would shake you. I might
Cover your head with a pillow or stuff a sock
Inside your mouth. This is one of the reasons
I cannot let you near me. Here are the others:
1.) I cannot stand the way you smell. The odors
Of the foods digesting in your stomach, coming up

Through your breath and the pores of your skin,
Or the scents you might wear to hide them,
The sweet hills of the South of France or
The sandalwood of the East, sicken me, they
Remind me of places I would not want to go.
I like things devoid of fragrance or smelling
Like nothing in nature. I like the way things are
When they come back from the dry cleaners. If
You were near me, you would have to be dry cleaned.
2.) I cannot tolerate movement. One night when I was
Small, I stayed on my uncle's boat. The seiche
Of the lake, which others found so hospitable,
Made me vomit inside the case of my pillow.
I threw it overboard and denied I'd been given one.
I know that you will never be able to keep still.
3.) I hate the way hair feels. It has taken me
All my life to get used to the way my own
Hair feels. It is horrible to think it is alive,
Poking out through the skin, hurting like wires.
If you left one on the sheet I would scream. As if
These things were not enough, you would want to talk.
This I could not allow. Discourse is possible
For only the briefest of exchanges, the handling
Of money across a counter or simple comments
On the outlook of the weather. But no more.
I avoid the news, live TV, and talk radio.
I like voices best when they have been pre-recorded.

Someone has already listened and decided,
As I have decided in composing this message.
I am sorry if you believe I have deceived you,
But I will not respond to further correspondence.
That smile you say you saw me give when passing
Was, I assure you, accidental and should not be
Confused with anything but a speck in my eye
Or an angle of light. I must be more careful."

THE CHAMBER

"For years I waited for this to happen to me.
It was my precious secret, the affair I imagined
Before falling asleep. Then my dreams would
Terrify me. All night I swam in my sheets.
Sometimes thinking about the future, I would rise
In my office and knock the wooden door or the frame
Of the window. Looking down, I would see one
Rolling across the street or being pushed
With a patient smile. Then I would knock
Wood again. It went on this way for years.
People believed I was merely superstitious.
A funny little man with peculiar habits.
That's the way people treat artists. Yet,
I understood their behavior—I had nothing
To offer. Once I won a trip to London.
I went alone. I was grateful for the double seat
And even had the stewardess bring me double portions.
When we landed at Heathrow, I would not stand up.
I waited until the passengers left the plane
And still I would not stand up.
The stewardess asked if there was a problem.
When I told her she could not hear me.
I watched as she watched my lips and frowned.
An attendant came and lifted me into a wheelchair.

He chatted at me. I liked his British accent.
Near the baggage claim area I felt the urge
To rise. I don't remember what I told him
But he stopped the chair. He shouted for me
To stop but I broke into a trot, took my bag
From the carousel, and climbed into a taxi.
Everyone watched as I sped away. I was amazing.
That was the first of what are called episodes.
Others are less memorable yet always occurring
In some public place: a museum, a restaurant,
A restroom. And people always wanted to help.
I did not mean to disappoint them or refute
Their kindness. I can still see that dear, tricked
Look cloud their faces as I made my recovery.
But they were not relieved. I found myself
Told not to enter certain establishments,
The proprietors acting downright hostile.
I never said a word. I just lowered my head.
Eventually, I was fired from the firm where I worked.
My superiors believed I was no longer promising
And that I had a bad effect on the younger men
Just up from college. They called it retirement.
Now I am doing what I have always anticipated.

At night the various moths are attracted
To the light of the window. I draw them in my mind.
Here is the lesson I have learned from life:
I took the wrong road but finally came home.
I read somewhere about a statue inside
A stone. This is what I have done. My work
Of art. I have carved at myself these many years
While I have posed for a statue inside a stone."

HOUSEHOLD GODS

Some are rock and some are bark,
Some guard the door and some the hearth;
One stands watch in the rose garden.
All commemorate Place and Time.

This story the Etruscans were fond of drawing:
Aeneas with his father on his back
(Like a man wearing history into the world)
Carried Troy's gods to the Tiber's mouth.

A certain stone unearthed in the meadow
Braces the music upon the piano.
The stump that bears no leaves bears witness
To increase and cutting and the light of day.

These are our household gods,
Silent until we give them voices,
Homelier than those others that hover
To work mischief or test our faith.

First the dream, then the dream recalled,
Then, finally, the way the dream gets told.
A fissured egg made of alabaster
Waits on the sill to deliver our Helen.

THE RETIREMENT OF
THE TROUBADOUR

I

How simple the words seem,
Slight and well meant,
Not a crime but not an achievement,
He mourns for each of them.
When they came from him they were bright.
It is we who have tarnished them.

II

The subjects were the heart and hurt.
Hardly popular in any age.
No pity please. That life was sweet
As sleeping late. Women and men
At their various situations,
In language any fool could understand.

III

Cathedrals rising from the fields,
Those images spoke for themselves
And of the rooms he had inhabited,
Shrines to the demi- and full goddesses.
The smell of the sex on his body,
In the half-light his unsung aubades.

IV

He remembers the dark street and the sun
Just rising. Beloved demi-monde,
That life is gone. In his hand
The crescent moon of a broken saucer,
A torn admission to the domestic theatre.
Under his hat the memory of stars.

ACKNOWLEDGMENTS

Some of the poems in this collection first appeared in the following publications:

AGNI: "Buddies," "Fool's Gold," "Needs," and "Sand"
The Antioch Review: "For Robert Maurer"
Boston Review: "Cares" and "Souvenir"
The Gettysburg Review: "The Bulletin Board"
Graham House Review: "Between Two Storms"
The New Republic: "Household Gods"
New Virginia Review: "Good Hope Road"
Onthebus: "Cheats"
Partisan Review: "History Lessons"
Ploughshares: "Hates" and "Wishes"

Several selections were also published in *Animate Earth*, Jeanne Duval Editions, 1988.

My thanks are many and deep to my brother and to my friends.